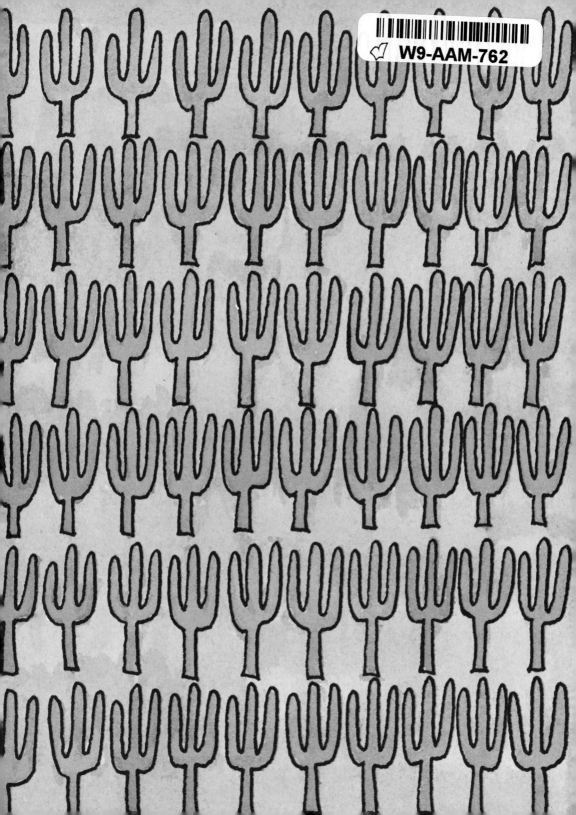

HENRY GOES WEST

by Robert Quackenbush

PARENTS MAGAZINE PRESS · NEW YORK

For Piet

A Parents Magazine
READ ALOUD AND EASY READING PROGRAM® Original.

Distributed in Canada by Clarke, Irwin & Co., Ltd.
Toronto, Canada

Library of Congress Cataloging in Publication Data.
Quackenbush, Robert M. Henry goes West.
SUMMARY: Lonely without his friend Clara who is
vacationing out West, Henry the Duck decides to
pay her a surprise visit.
[1. Ducks — Fiction.   2. West (U.S.) — Fiction.
3. Humorous stories]   I. Title.
PZ7.Q16Hc 1982 [E] 82-7971
ISBN 0-8193-1089-1 AACR2
ISBN 0-8193-1090-5 (lib. bdg.)

Henry the Duck missed
his friend Clara,
who was vacationing out West.
He decided to pay her
a surprise visit.
So he packed his bag
and took the first plane
heading West to meet her.

Henry arrived at
Clara's guest ranch
early the next morning.
But the ranch was closed.
Everyone had just left
for an all-day trail ride.
They would not be back
until midnight.

Henry decided to
have a look around
the ranch while he
waited for Clara.
As he was snapping a picture
near the barn,
Henry backed right into a mule.

The surprised mule
kicked Henry!
Henry landed on
the back of a horse.

The horse was a
bucking bronco!
Henry was taken
for a wild ride.
Then he was tossed
over a fence.

Henry landed in a bull's pen!
The bull chased Henry.
Henry ran and ran.

At last Henry got out
of the bull's pen.
He went to sit
on a large rock.
But he did not see
the cactus behind it.
Henry sat down
on the cactus!

Henry jumped up
and quacked loudly.
The noise frightened
some cattle
grazing nearby.

The cattle began running.
Soon they were racing
at full speed.
Henry had started
a stampede!

Henry escaped to the hills
in the nick of time.
He pulled the
cactus stickers
from his tail.
Then he headed
back to the ranch.

On the way, Henry
spotted an unusual rock.
He thought it would make
a good present for Clara.
But as soon as he
picked up the rock…

he heard a loud rumbling
from the mountaintop.
Henry had started
a landslide!
He ran as fast as
he could go.

Henry got clear
of the landslide.
Then he went straight back
to the ranch
to wait for Clara.

Henry waited and waited.
It was turning cold
on the desert.
So Henry built a campfire.
He stood close to the fire
to warm his tail feathers.
Too close.

Suddenly, Henry's
tail feathers
began to sizzle!
He made a beeline
for the water
and dove in.

Henry was soaking wet
and all worn out.
He wished Clara would hurry up
and get there.

At last the riding party returned.
But Clara was not with them.
Henry asked one of the cowboys
if he had seen her.

"Sorry, mister," said
the cowboy...

"Clara went home yesterday.
She said she was lonesome
for someone named Henry."

ABOUT THE AUTHOR

When ROBERT QUACKENBUSH manages to get away from the city, he usually finds himself on what he calls a "Henry-the-Duck-vacation." That means his plane flight is cancelled, his hotel forgets to keep his room for him, and it rains every single day he's away. But Mr. Quackenbush has that rare ability to turn a disaster into a funny story. And so, Parents is pleased to add *Henry Goes West* to the popular Henry the Duck series.

Mr. Quackenbush is the author/artist of more than 100 books for children. He has been awarded honors and prizes, and recently was nominated for the Edgar Allen Poe Award in the juvenile category. His artwork has been exhibited in leading museums across the U.S. and is now on display in the gallery he owns and runs in New York City. He also teaches writing and illustrating there.

Mr. Quackenbush, who is a native of Arizona, now lives in New York City with his wife, Margery, and their son, Piet.

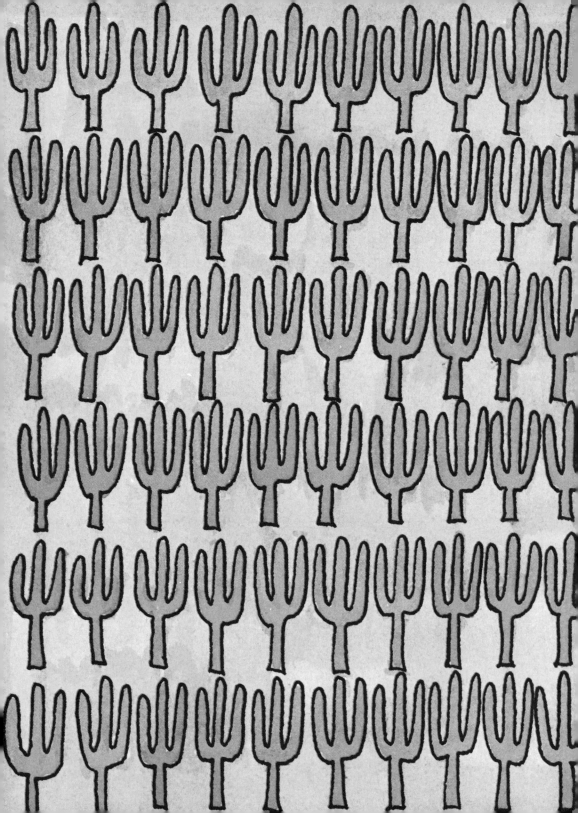